Fleabag

Jan Weeks

ILLUSTRATED BY

Alex Tyers

Nelson

chapter **one**

I wanted a dog but my parents
wouldn't let me have one. The house we
rented was too small. It had a backyard
the size of a postage stamp. There wasn't
enough room for humans, let alone dogs.

"I don't mind if it's a small dog," I said. It made no difference. No dog!

They said when we moved I could have any dog I liked. As if we ever would! We had more chance of winning lotto. Every time my parents saved any money, something happened, like the car breaking down, or my sister needing braces on her teeth.

My sister's name is Kate. She's a year older than me. If the opportunity ever arose, I'd swap her for a dog.

"Why don't you pretend to own one," she suggested. "That way it wouldn't cost you anything to feed it."

"Why don't you pretend to own a brain," I answered. "That way someone might think you have one. But I don't know who."

According to Dad, dogs need a big yard.
Dogs need exercise. He's right about the
exercise. My dog would get lots going
for walks after school.

Dogs also need someone to love and care
for them. I'd be good at that.

Every kid should have a pet. It teaches you to be responsible. Child experts tell you that. Without a pet, how could I be expected to grow into a responsible adult?

I needed a dog.

He was sitting in a cage in the pet shop, looking sad and lonely. He saw me and his puppy tail began to wag.

When I picked him up, he licked me. First on my hand, then my face. You could tell we were meant for each other.

The sign above his cage said "Free to a Good Home". Free! I couldn't believe my luck.

meant

"Mine's a good home," I rushed to tell Mrs Sims, the shop owner. I was in her shop so often I was almost a fixture.

"You're sure your parents won't mind, Rick?" she answered. "Puppies take a bit of looking after."

"Of course not!" I lied. "Dad's always saying I should have a dog."

I was going to smuggle him into the house, hide him in my wardrobe and hope they never discovered that he was there.

Mrs Sims didn't know what kind of dog he was. A bit of this and a bit of something else. One thing was sure, he was no pure-breed.

Someone had left him in Mrs Sims'
backyard. She'd heard this yelping noise
coming from a box just inside the gate.
When she went to investigate, there he
was, cold, hungry and whimpering for his
mum.

"He'd be lucky to be eight weeks old,"
she said. "I think it's criminal to leave a
pup like that."

I was ever so grateful. At last I was
going to have a dog of my own.

"I'll take good care of him, Mrs Sims," I
promised. "You won't be sorry you gave
him to me."

chapter two

"**T**hat's the ugliest pup I ever saw," Kate said.

It was useless trying to keep a secret from her. Not when her nose was always in my business.

"Which bit of him is ugly?" I asked. I was sitting on my bed, playing with him.

"Every bit," she answered. "He looks more like a wombat than a dog."

That was true. With his grey coat and thick body, he could've been mistaken for a baby wombat.

"What are you going to call him?" Kate asked.

It might not be a bad idea, I decided, to let her choose the name. That way she'd be less likely to tell Mum and Dad.

"Fred's a good name," she said.

Fred! What kind of name was that? What was wrong with Fang or Brutus?

"We'll call him Fred if you promise not to tell Mum and Dad that I have him."

"Fat chance!" she answered. I might've guessed it wouldn't be that easy. If I wanted Kate's silence, I'd have to pay for it. I could start by doing the dishes by myself. "And you can put the garbage out," she added.

That was blackmail, I complained. She agreed.

"Wait until you want something," I grumbled.

Doing the dishes was no fun. Mum used every saucepan and Dad burnt everything.

"You're the one who wants the ugly dog," Kate said.

It was easy to see why we didn't get along.

I really did expect Fred to settle in his box in the wardrobe and go to sleep. He should've been exhausted after all the attention I'd given him.

He wasn't hungry either. His stomach was crammed full of the steak and kidney I'd dropped into a plastic bag during dinner.

Fred had other ideas. He wanted to be with me. There was so much noise coming from the wardrobe, it was a wonder my parents didn't hear.

In the end, I decided to put him in the bed beside me. Before you could say "Fred" he was asleep.

When I woke up, he was licking my face. During the night he'd wet on me. Not once but lots of times. My pyjamas felt damp and clung to my skin.

He'd wet on me, the pillow, the sheet. It had even gone through the sheet to soak into the mattress.

When I put him on the floor, he did another lot on the carpet.

Then, horror of horrors, he did something worse!

About then, Kate poked her nose into my room. "Pretend you did it," she said, looking at my bed.

As if Mum was going to believe that! I was two the last time I'd wet the bed.

chapter three

It smelt so bad when I was cleaning the carpet, I was almost sick.

"Oh yuck!" I said, feeling my stomach churn. I was holding my nose, using a pair of underpants as a cleaning rag.

After that I had to clean the underpants. Running into the toilet, I hung onto them with two fingers, before pushing the flush button.

When I looked, they were gone. I hoped
Mum wouldn't miss them. I hoped they
wouldn't clog the pipes.

Back in my room, I grabbed the sheets,
tossing them into the corner. Fred sat on
top, thinking we were playing a game.
He looked so cute, I couldn't stay mad
with him.

Pouring disinfectant onto the wet patches,
I used Mum's hair dryer on the mattress.
It sort of worked but I was running out
of time.

About then, I had this good idea. I
decided to turn the mattress over. "Clever
boy!" I said to myself.

With the sheets in my arms, I raced downstairs, past Mum, who was cooking breakfast, into the laundry.

"How long is it since you changed my sheets?" I asked, opening the washing machine's lid to drop them in. "They smell awful."

Making Mum feel guilty was always a good form of defence.

"I was going to change your sheets today," Mum answered. She was so busy working in the cake shop, things like that often slipped her mind. Dad never thought about them at all.

"I bet they've been on my bed for a year," I said.

"Hardly!" she answered. "What's to stop you changing the sheets anyway? I don't see your hands tied behind your back."

"That's what I am doing," I answered, stopping to grab a piece of toast.

I should eat a proper breakfast, I was told. I had soccer training, I lied. If I was late, they'd put me out of the team.

That'd already happened, but I had more important things than breakfast to worry about.

I had to decide what to do about Fred. Should I take him to school and pretend I'd brought him to show the class in Science?

My teacher would never let me get away with it. Besides, we wrote a day-to-day account of our lives in diary form.

If I left him in my bedroom, he wouldn't like it. And Mum didn't go to work until ten. She'd hear him.

"What do you think I should do, Kate?" I asked.

"Spray him with invisible ink," she answered. "That'd give Mum something to think about."

I don't know why I bothered to talk to Kate. She was never any help.

In the end I opted to hide him in the garden shed. Owning a dog was no simple matter.

chapter four

I got away with it for almost three days. Then old Mrs Hobbs came back from her holiday. She was our next-door neighbour.

"I don't have a dog myself," she said, "so I don't see why I should have to put up with someone else's."

She was standing on our doorstep in her pink dressing-gown and red slippers. It was only seven o'clock and she was ready for bed.

Mum and Dad looked at her as if she was crazy. Not because she was complaining. She did that all the time. It was the dog bit that baffled them.

"It's done nothing but carry on all day," Mrs Hobbs continued. "And me an old lady!"

"What has?" Dad asked. She'd waited for him to come home from work.

"Your dog!"

"We don't have a dog!" Mum said.

"Then tell me what's been making that racket in your garden shed."

"Say it's your pet hippopotamus," Kate whispered.

It was time for me to confess. Standing with Fred in my arms, I said, "Mrs Sims gave him to me. She was going to send him to the pound." Tears welled in my eyes and I did my best to look pathetic. "He's only a little pup."

"Little pups grow into big dogs," Mrs Hobbs said. "I don't want a dog next door. He'll have to go."

"Is that so?" Dad answered, more annoyed with Mrs Hobbs than with me. "In this house we make the decisions, Mrs Hobbs, not you! The dog stays."

I was so grateful to Mrs Hobbs, I could've kissed her. Well, almost!

Off went Mrs Hobbs in a huff, threatening to call the police if Fred so much as barked. It was against the law, we were told, to keep a noisy animal.

"You know what's happened?" Mum said. "You've given Rick permission to keep a dog."

Dad nodded, realising what he'd done.

"He deserves to be punished," Mum went on, "not rewarded."

I was getting ready to cry again.

"You're right," Dad agreed. "Get to your bedroom, Rick."

"You should make him do the dishes for a month," put in Kate. Trust her!

I was also to be grounded for a month. The last bit was to satisfy Mum. In a day or two it'd be forgotten. At least I didn't have to take Fred back to the pet shop.

He was to stay downstairs. In the kitchen, Mum decided, where there was lino on the floor.

"Odd-looking little thing, isn't he?" I heard her say as I climbed the stairs. "I hope he doesn't grow too big."

Later, when I went downstairs to get a glass of milk, I found Fred asleep on Dad's lap in the lounge room.

"He was lonely in the kitchen," Dad said.

chapter **five**

a dog had bitten Mum when she was a little girl. She'd never forgiven it and held all dogs responsible. That included Fred.

Mum had him toilet-trained within a week. Every time he made a mess, she'd push him outside with the mop.

"Ugly, dirty little thing!" she'd growl. "Do your business somewhere else."

Finding a flea on her lounge, she called him Fleabag and wouldn't let him back in the house at all.

As Fred grew older, Dad renamed him Houdini. He kept escaping through holes he had dug under the fence. He wouldn't come back when called, and I spent half my time looking for him.

"Ugly *and* deaf," Kate said.

His favourite place was Mrs Hobbs' garden. Whenever she saw him, she'd yell at him. Or hose him. Or throw things at him. Fred didn't care. He'd just wait a while, then sneak back in to help himself to her cat's dinner.

One day he pulled a petticoat off her clothesline. I caught him dragging it into our yard. By then it had holes in it and was all muddy.

Mrs Hobbs would've been mad if she'd seen him. Fortunately she hadn't so I wrapped it in newspaper and threw it in the bin.

Another day Fred dug up Mrs Hobbs' pansies. They were just starting to flower. She was out in her car. I had to replant every one of them. They never looked any good after that.

Everybody in the neighbourhood knew Fred. He visited them all. Off he'd go on his short little legs, down the centre of the road, tail wagging, never doubting his welcome.

They had a pet show at school. I entered Fred. I should've had more sense. Not because he didn't win. It was because I could no longer pretend he wasn't mine when he came strolling into the classroom.

Scratch, scratch, scratch! Fred was always scratching. Fleas loved him. We couldn't get rid of them. Mum had the backyard fumigated so often, it's a wonder we weren't all exterminated.

It had to do with the company Fred kept. The dirtier the dog, the more Fred liked it.

We tried keeping him in the yard. Dad tied him to the barbecue. Fred spent half the day chewing through the gas hose. Realising his mistake, he spent the rest of it chomping through the rope.

Chained up instead, Fred complained so loudly that Mrs Hobbs was back on our doorstep. Fred had been giving her cat a hard time as well.

"Pity she has so little to do with her time," Dad said.

chapter **six**

One day Fred disappeared. He didn't come home for his dinner. I spent hours going up and down the streets, whistling and calling his name.

I asked everyone if they'd seen him but nobody had. Dad and Mum went out in the car. There was no sign of him.

"He'll turn up," Dad said, but he didn't.

"Maybe he's found some place he likes better," Kate said.

I kept looking over Mrs Hobbs' fence, wondering if she'd done something to him.

"Fred's gone," I said, glaring at her. "We can't find him anywhere."

"Too bad," she answered, but I knew she didn't mean it. She even offered me a chocolate bar.

Five lonely days went past. Mrs Sims let me put a reward notice in her window. Dad rang the newspaper. It didn't do any good. Fred had vanished.

On the fifth night, Dad pulled up, tooting his car horn. I raced out and there was Fred, sitting in the front seat.

"The dog catcher caught him," Dad said. "I found him at the pound."

He'd told them he was looking for an ugly dog, not unlike a wombat. They knew right away they had him. There couldn't be another dog which looked like that.

It didn't bother me that others thought he was ugly. I was just glad to have him back.

"You paid *how much* to get him out of the pound?" Mum asked, her eyes bulging.

They bulged even further when Dad told her he had had to pay for a dog licence as well.

I only kept Fred for six months after he came back from the pound.

Mrs Hobbs backed into him. She was reversing out of her drive.

I was in my bedroom when I heard the squeal of brakes. Then I heard Fred. He was yelping with pain. Then he stopped.

When I raced outside, he was on the footpath. Blood was trickling out of his mouth. I could see he was having trouble breathing.

"You've run over Fred," I cried.

"It was an accident," Mrs Hobbs answered, her eyes filling with tears. "He ran behind the car. I didn't know he was there."

"He's dying!"

"I hope not. Oh Rick, I'm so sorry!"

My parents were at work. Mrs Hobbs lifted Fred into her car then drove to the vet's. He was dead before we got there.

We held the funeral in Mrs Hobbs' backyard. She said I could bury him in her pansy garden. Fred would've liked that.

We stood around his grave, tossing handfuls of dirt onto the box Dad had made.

"Bye, Fred!" I said. "Bye, Fleabag! You were the best dog a kid could've had!"

Mrs Hobbs offered to buy me another one, but I shook my head. I didn't want another dog.